Oliver
Twist

Acknowledgments
Artists Penko Gelev
Sotir Gelev

First edition for North America (including Canada and Mexico), Philippine Islands, and Puerto Rico published in 2006 by Barron's Educational Series, Inc.

All inquiries should be addressed to:
Barron's Educational Series, Inc.
250 Wireless Boulevard
Hauppauge, NY 11788
www.barronseduc.com

ISBN-13 (Hardcover): 978-0-7641-5975-6
ISBN-10 (Hardcover): 0-7641-5975-5
ISBN-13 (Paperback): 978-0-7641-3490-6
ISBN-10 (Paperback): 0-7641-3490-6

Library of Congress Control No.: 2005936253

Printed and bound in China
9 8 7 6 5 4 3 2 1

Oliver Twist

Charles Dickens

Illustrated by
Penko Gelev

Retold by
John Malam

Series created and designed by
David Salariya

After a few struggles, Oliver breathed, sneezed, and proceeded to advertise to the inmates of the workhouse the fact of a new burden having been imposed on the parish, by setting up as loud a cry as could reasonably have been expected . . .

Charles Dickens, *Oliver Twist.*

CHARACTERS

Oliver Twist

Fagin,
leader of a gang of
thieves

Bill Sikes,
a violent thief

Nancy,
Bill's girlfriend

Mr. Brownlow

The Artful Dodger
(Jack Dawkins)

Rose Maylie

Mr. Bumble

Monks,
a mysterious figure

Sally Thingummy

Mr. Grimwig

Mrs. Bedwin,
Mr. Brownlow's housekeeper

Mrs. Maylie

Mrs. Corney, (later
becomes Mrs. Bumble)

Noah Claypole

Dr. Losberne

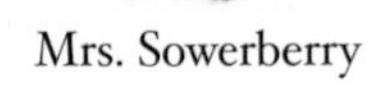

Mrs. Sowerberry

Mr. Sowerberry,
an undertaker

Toby Crackit

Charlotte,
Noah's girlfriend

Charley Bates

Oliver Twist is Born

Here is the sorry tale of Oliver Twist, a child born in the workhouse.[1] At birth he struggled to breathe, and the surgeon was sure he would die.

But Oliver's lungs were strong, and as he began to cry, his mother called for him. Sally Thingummy, a drunken old nurse, stood at her bedside.

Oliver's mother pressed her cold lips to his forehead, fell back, and died. He was an orphan.

Oliver was farmed with other children at a branch workhouse.[2] On his eighth birthday he was locked in the cellar for daring to be hungry.

That same day, Mr. Bumble, the beadle, came for him.[3] Oliver was now old enough to be moved to the adult workhouse.

With a slice of bread in his hand, Oliver was led away from the wretched home of his infant years.

The main workhouse was a very strict place. Within minutes of arriving, Mr. Bumble took Oliver to meet the board of officials. They would decide what to do with him.

Oliver cried as he listened to his fate.

At six the next morning he began to pick oakum as the board instructed.[4]

1. Workhouse: A large public building where the poor were housed in return for work. See pp.44-46 for more information.
2. Farmed: Until they were about eight years old, infants were raised by a matron in a branch workhouse for children.
3. Beadle: A minor official responsible for keeping order and punishing offenders.
4. Pick oakum: Untwisting old rope to make loose fibers (oakum) for use on ships. It was a common task given to workhouse inmates.

In the Workhouse

At meal times Oliver lined up with the other children for a small bowl of gruel.[1] It was the only food, and there was never enough.

Oliver and the others suffered the tortures of slow starvation. One boy said he was so hungry he would eat the boy who slept next to him. The boys gave Oliver a task.

No one had ever dared ask for more! The master shrieked loudly for Mr. Bumble, who took the news of Oliver's bad behavior to the board.

The board was horrified and decided to make an example of Oliver. They ordered him to be locked up.

The board decided to sell Oliver for five pounds[2] to any man or woman who wanted an apprentice.[3]

ONE WEEK LATER . . .

A notice was pinned to the workhouse gate offering Oliver for sale. It was there for a week, and then Mr. Gamfield, a chimneysweep, saw it.[5]

The magistrates considered whether the sweep could buy Oliver.[6] But Oliver didn't want to go with the dreadful man. He'd rather be sent back to the workhouse. Luckily, the magistrates agreed not to let Oliver be sold.

1. Gruel: Thin porridge made from water (or milk) and oatmeal.
2. Five pounds: about ten dollars
3. Apprentice: A person who is learning how to do a job.
4. "I wants a 'prentis": Charles Dickens often wrote the way that people actually spoke. See p.46 for more information.
5. Chimneysweep: Someone who cleans the inside of chimneys.
6. Magistrates: Officials who make decisions in a local court.
7. Indentures: An agreement that binds an apprentice to a master.

Mr. Bumble tried unsuccessfully to find a ship that would take Oliver far away to sea. Then, as he returned to the workhouse, he met Mr. Sowerberry, the parish undertaker.[1]

That evening, Oliver was taken before the board for the last time. They informed him of his fate. Oliver was to leave the workhouse that very night, go to the coffinmaker's and work as his new house-lad.[2]

Oliver cried as Mr. Bumble led him away from the workhouse, and marched him off to Mr. Sowerberry's premises.

The undertaker's wife opened a side door, and pushed Oliver downstairs into a dark, damp room next to the coal cellar.[3]

Oliver was given scraps of cold meat that were meant for the Sowerberry's dog.

Oliver ate his poor supper, then followed Mrs. Sowerberry upstairs to a room full of coffins. She told him to sleep under the counter. The tiny, narrow bed looked like a grave. With a heavy heart, Oliver lay down to sleep.

1. Undertaker: Someone who arranges funerals.
2. House-lad: A child servant.
3. Coal cellar: Many houses had cellars to store coal.

Runaway!

Oliver was woken by a kick at the shop door. It was Noah Claypole, Mr. Sowerberry's shop-boy.[1]

Charlotte, the servant girl, treated Noah to a good breakfast. Oliver was given only stale leftovers, which he ate in the coldest corner of the room.

In the street, Noah was called names by other shop-boys. This made him angry, and he took it out on Oliver. From the very start, Noah bullied him.

After a month, Mr. Sowerberry hit upon an idea. He believed Oliver would make a good mute, and promised to train him for the job.[3]

When Mr. Sowerberry was next called upon to attend to a funeral, he took Oliver with him. It was the body of a poor woman, and as her coffin was hastily carried to the churchyard, Oliver did his best to walk ahead in silence.

Meanwhile, in the shop, Noah teased Oliver, and Charlotte copied him. One day, Noah tried to make Oliver cry. He taunted him with cruel words.

But Noah went too far with his taunts, and Oliver flew into a violent rage. He grabbed Noah by the throat and shook him hard.

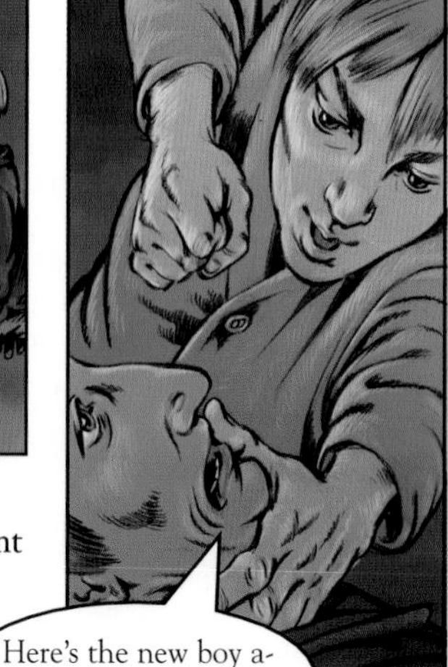

1. Shop-boy: An assistant.
2. D'ye hear, work'us?: 'Workhouse' was an insult Noah used on Oliver.
3. Mute: A person who leads a funeral procession in silence.

Hearing Noah's shouts, Mrs. Sowerberry and Charlotte ran into the kitchen screaming.

Charlotte ran to Noah's side and cradled him in her arms. She glared at Oliver, then in an instant, she leapt at him.

She grabbed Oliver and began to beat him. Mrs. Sowerberry scratched at him, and Noah attacked him from behind. There was nothing poor Oliver could do.

The beating over, Oliver was locked in the cellar, and finally sent to bed. In the still of the night he wept.

At first light, Oliver ran away from the coffin-maker's. He hid behind hedges, then set off again, and so on until noon.

For seven days, Oliver walked the long road to London. He slept under hayricks and begged for money.[1] His legs ached and his feet were sore from walking.

In the town of Barnet, a boy about the same age as Oliver approached him. He seemed friendly, and gave him food.

The boy, Jack Dawkins, said friends called him "The Artful Dodger." He was going to London that night, and Oliver could come with him.

It was dark when the boys reached the city. At an old house, the Dodger whistled a signal, and the boys entered.

1. Hayricks: Haystacks; piles of hay stacked for storing.
2. Covey: Victorian slang word for a man.
3. What's the row?: Victorian expression meaning "What's the matter?"
4. Lodgings: A place to stay.

Meeting New Friends

Jack led Oliver upstairs to a room at the back of the house. Inside was a shrivelled old man cooking sausages over a fire, and four or five boys.

The man with the villanous-looking face was Fagin. He gave Oliver, Jack and the others their supper. Fagin poured Oliver a glass of water and hot gin.[1]

The gin made Oliver tired. He was soon fast asleep in Fagin's den, on a rough bed made of old sacks.

Next day, as Oliver awoke to the sound of Fagin muttering, he saw the old gentleman take a gold pocket-watch from a box full of jewelry.

Fagin had thought that Oliver was sleeping, but when his dark eyes saw that the boy had been watching him, he slammed the lid down on the box.

Oliver admitted he'd seen the pretty things, and Fagin, saying they were his, hid the box.

The Dodger entered the room with Charley Bates, another of Fagin's lads. As they talked about some sort of work, Fagin gave Oliver a sly look.

Dodger handed the pocketbooks over to Fagin, and Charley gave him four silk handkerchiefs.[4] Fagin was very pleased.

1. Gin: A strong alcoholic drink. Oliver drank it diluted with water.
2. Clever dogs! Fine fellows!: Fagin is talking about the boys who work for him.
3. Pocketbooks were what gentlemen carried their money in.
4. Handkerchief: A large square of expensive silk carried by Victorian gentlemen; their initials were embroidered into them.

Oliver wanted to learn their work, so he watched as Fagin pretended to be a gentleman in the street. Dodger and Charley walked close behind him.

Fagin stopped, as he might have done had he been looking into a shop window. The boys stopped too, watching him, careful not to be seen.

And then they did it. The Dodger distracted him, and in an instant Fagin's pockets were picked clean.

The boys helped themselves to a pocket-watch, wallet, snuff-box, handkerchief, and spectacles case.[1]

Fagin turned to Oliver, praising the boys' work. He urged Oliver to follow their example, adding that he would become a great man if he did.

Then he set Oliver a test—to take a handkerchief from his pocket without him noticing, as Dodger and Charley had done. Oliver thought it was a game.

For the next week, Oliver unpicked initials from the handkerchiefs. It seemed an odd sort of work.[2]

When he wasn't unpicking initials from the handkerchiefs the Dodger and Charley brought home, he played Fagin's curious game.

But Fagin was not as kind he had seemed, and when the other boys arrived empty-handed from their work, he grew angry and sent them to bed hungry.

1. Snuff-box: A small container for holding snuff (powdered tobacco).
2. This was so that Fagin could sell the valuable silk.

MISTAKEN IDENTITY

Oliver was keen to learn what sort of work his new friends did for Fagin, so one day he went with them. On their way to work, Charley stole an apple from a stall.

He couldn't imagine what their work was, especially as they seemed to be wandering without purpose—until the Dodger stopped them at a bookstall.

The boys observed a gentleman at the bookstall. Oliver was surprised by their behavior.

Then the Dodger and Charley stepped up close to the gentleman. Oliver followed a few paces behind, and looked on in silent amazement.

The gentleman was so busy reading a book, page after page, that he didn't notice the boys at all.

But they had seen him, and the Dodger knew exactly what to do next as he took a handkerchief from the man's pocket and gave it to Charley.

So it was that in an instant Oliver understood what work his friends did, and wanting to get away, he ran.

Realizing his misfortune, the gentleman turned, saw Oliver running away and thought him the thief.

People stopped what they were doing, and their calls of "Stop, thief!" filled poor Oliver's ears as he tried to escape the scene of the crime.

1. Prime plant: A target; a good choice to pick.

Oliver ran fast, and sweat rolled down his face. Exhausted, he was caught! The crowd held him tightly until the gentleman arrived.

The gentleman said Oliver was indeed the thief. He saw that Oliver was hurt, and seemed sorry for him.

Oliver was taken to the judge for punishment. The gentleman, who said his name was Brownlow, explained it all.

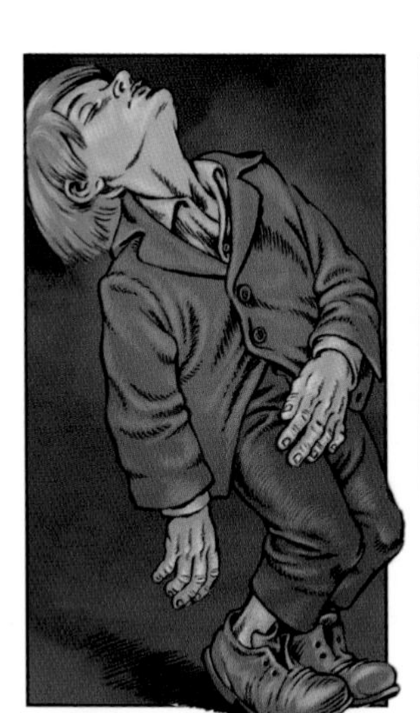

Stop—don't take him away.

Poor Oliver fainted, and while he lay on the floor the magistrate sentenced him to three months' hard labor.[1] Then, as he was being taken away, a stranger shouted.

It was the bookseller, who said he'd seen another boy rob Mr. Brownlow. Oliver was free, but was now very ill.

Mr. Brownlow took pity on Oliver, who had a bad fever. He put him to bed in his house, and he slept for days.

In Oliver's room there was a portrait of a lady. For some reason, he kept staring at it.

Mr. Brownlow noticed that Oliver resembled the lady in the painting. This was a surprise to them both.

1. Hard labor was often given as punishment to criminals.

ENTER BILL SIKES

After the incident at the bookstall, the Dodger and Charley returned to Fagin. He heard them on the stairs . . .

The Dodger wriggled out of his coat and snatched the toasting-fork.[2] He jabbed it at Fagin, who stepped back.

Fagin seized a beer bottle and made to throw it at the Dodger—but Charley let out a howl and the old man aimed it in his direction instead.

The bottle missed Charley. It flew right across the room, spilling its beer over Bill Sikes who nobody had seen enter. He was a scruffy sight.

Sikes, who was Fagin's partner in crime, called to his dog. A shaggy creature skulked into the room.

Here was a man of violence that even Fagin seemed afraid of. When Sikes demanded a glass of spirits, Fagin obediently poured one for him.[3]

Sikes listened to the boys' story. He was concerned that Oliver had been arrested, because if he spoke about them, the gang would be in trouble.

1. Traps: Term used by Victorian criminals for "police."
2. Toasting-fork: Large metal fork used to hold food while it was cooking.
3. Spirits: Strong alcohol, such as gin or whisky.

Sikes and Fagin decided someone should go to the police station to find out if Oliver had spoken about them. After much arguing, they sent Nancy, who was a friend of the gang.

Nancy pretended she was looking for her little brother. An officer explained that Oliver had been released, because he was found innocent. He told her that Mr. Brownlow had taken Oliver.

She made her way back to Fagin's secret hideaway, careful not to be followed there. The gang listened as Nancy gave them the news of what had happened to Oliver.

Sikes was the first to react to the news. He called to his dog and rushed from the room, without so much as a "goodbye" to the others.

Fagin issued instructions to the rest of his gang, telling them to search for Oliver and report back to him. Pushing them from the room, Fagin locked the door, then filled his pockets with stolen jewelry from his secret box.

A Den of Thieves

A week after the affair of the picture, Mr. Brownlow asked Oliver how he had fallen into bad company. Oliver cried as he began to tell his sorry tale.

No sooner had Oliver started, than he was interrupted by the arrival of Mr. Grimwig, a friend of Mr. Brownlow's. He clearly knew all about Oliver from his friend.

Oliver bowed to Mr. Grimwig, who nodded with good humor and then asked how he was.

Mr. Brownlow had decided that Oliver was a trustworthy boy. He sent him on an errand to the bookseller, to return some books and pay for some others.

Mr. Grimwig, on the other hand, thought Oliver could not be trusted. He didn't expect him to return to Mr. Brownlow.

The errand should only have taken a few minutes, but Oliver took a wrong turn . . . and had the misfortune to be spotted by Nancy.

A crowd gathered, and Nancy said Oliver was a runaway. Oliver tried to explain the truth, but no one listened. Bill Sikes arrived and, after striking poor Oliver on the head, dragged him back to Fagin's den.

1. Shilling: A coin used in Britain in the 19th century.

As Fagin and the others poked fun at Oliver about his new suit of clothes, the Dodger found the five-pound note in Oliver's pocket and took it.

Fagin and Sikes saw it too, and each man claimed it was theirs. It ended up with Sikes, who told Fagin he could have the books.

Oliver fell to his knees at Fagin's feet, and pleaded with him to send the money and books back to Mr. Brownlow.

Fagin listened to Oliver's pitiful words, then, narrowing his eyes and rubbing his hands, he stared at Oliver.

It was too much for Oliver to bear. He jumped to his feet and ran to the door, but there was to be no escape for him.

Fagin took Oliver and hit him on the shoulder. He was about to strike again, but Nancy cried out for him to stop. Fagin told Oliver about a boy who had betrayed him to the police in the past, and was hanged.

By now Nancy regretted helping to catch Oliver. She felt sorry for him. Charley Bates swapped Oliver's smart new clothes for his old ones, then locked the door leaving him in the dark. Soon Oliver was playing the "game" again.

A Face from the Past

There came a time when Mr. Bumble, the beadle, travelled to London on workhouse business. He had a surprise when he read the London newspaper.

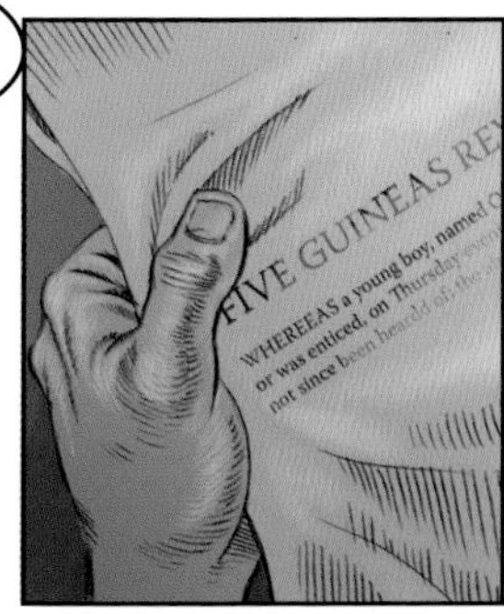

There, before his eyes, was an advertisement from Mr. Brownlow asking for information on Oliver Twist.

The writer of the ad asked for Oliver's history which, of course, Mr. Bumble knew very well. He called on Mr. Brownlow without further delay.

The beadle was shown into a back room, where Mr. Brownlow and his friend, Mr. Grimwig, were sitting. Mr. Brownlow invited Mr. Bumble to sit with them, moved a lamp so he could see the visitor more clearly, then asked him what he knew about Oliver.

Mr. Bumble told how Oliver was an orphan raised in the workhouse, had attacked Noah, and had run away.

Mr. Brownlow had hoped to hear a good account of the boy, but the beadle's sorry story made him think Oliver was a little villain after all and he was sorry to have trusted him.

1. Foundling: A child that is found and whose parents are unknown.
2. Imposter: A person pretending to be something they are not.

One cold, windy night, a few weeks after Oliver had been caught by the gang, Fagin set off to visit Bill Sikes at his house. The two thieves had serious business to discuss.

Fagin knocked on the door, and a dog growled from inside. A man's voice demanded to know who was there. Fagin turned the door handle and let himself in, and was greeted by Bill Sikes and Nancy.

Fagin and Sikes were soon deep in conversation. They talked about a house burglary they were planning to do, and what they needed for the job.

As soon as Nancy heard Sikes asking for a boy, she urged Fagin to remind him about Oliver.

Fagin told Sikes that Oliver was the boy for the job. He was the right size and he'd do everything he was told—as long as he was frightened.

Fagin returned to his gloomy den, and over breakfast the next day he told Oliver what was to become of him—he was to be handed over to Bill Sikes.

Late that night, Nancy came for Oliver. She held his hand tightly, and led him out into the dark street.

1. Big 'un: Small boys were most useful to criminals as they could climb through very small windows.

The Burglary

Sikes made Oliver stand in front of him. The robber waved a loaded pistol at Oliver, and threatened to shoot him if he dared to speak without permission.

Early the next day, Sikes dragged Oliver through the streets of London. They took a ride in a cart out of the city, then walked to a public house.[1]

At the pub they ate and rested their weary legs, and Sikes smoked his pipe. Sikes asked a fellow traveller for a lift in his cart and he agreed.

They rode for miles, then walked on to join up with Toby Crackit, as Sikes had arranged. The thieves, with Oliver in tow, then set off to do their work.

Oh! for God's sake let me go!

Now, for the first time, Oliver knew what their work was to be. Terrified, he fell to his knees, but Sikes picked him up and threatened him with the pistol.

Crackit knocked the pistol from Sikes' grasp and grabbed hold of Oliver. He put his hand over the boy's mouth and dragged him toward the house.

At the back of the house, Sikes opened a small window, which was just the right size for Oliver to squeeze through.

1. Public house: a bar.
2. Strew your brains: Spread Oliver's brain over the grass.

Sikes lowered Oliver through the window, telling him to make his way to the front door and open it so that he and Crackit could enter the house.

As soon as Oliver was inside, he decided to alert the house. Seeing him going for the stairs, Sikes shouted and a startled Oliver dropped his lantern. Suddenly men appeared upstairs!

Sikes cried out for Oliver to come back. A shot was fired inside the house. Sikes fired back, then pulled Oliver out of the window. He'd been wounded!

Crackit and Sikes, with Oliver unconscious in his arms, ran from the house, chased by men and dogs. Oliver slowed Sikes down, and it wasn't long before Crackit was racing ahead.

The shout from Sikes brought Crackit to a stop and he returned. They laid Oliver in a ditch, then ran at great speed, jumping hedges and crossing fields. Not for the first time in his life, Oliver had been abandoned.

1. White-livered hound: Coward.

A Confession

As the break-in was taking place, a happier event was happening for Mr. Bumble. He called on Mrs. Corney, a widow, and the matron of the workhouse where Oliver had been born.

Mr. Bumble and Mrs. Corney chatted over cups of tea and toast, and it was clear they liked each other a lot. They were interrupted by an old woman who brought grave news about Sally Thingummy's health.

The old woman said Sally had something of importance to say to Mrs. Corney before she died. The old woman hobbled to Sally's room and Mrs. Corney followed.

Sally told Mrs. Corney about the night she nursed a woman who gave birth to a child, then died. The woman had entrusted Sally with her gold locket.

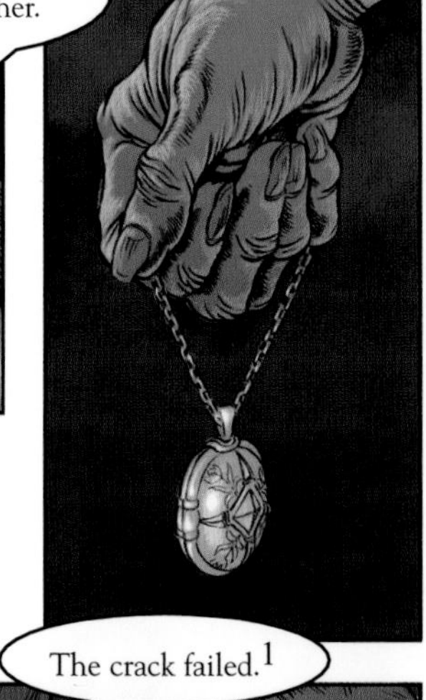

They called
him Oliver.

With her last breath, Sally explained how the locket would lead to people who would care for the woman's child. Mrs. Corney asked for the child's name.

Meanwhile . . .

The crack failed.[1]

As the truth of Oliver's birth was coming out at the workhouse, Fagin was learning the bad news from the newspapers and Toby Crackit about the robbery.

1. Crack: Victorian slang word for a robbery.

Crackit told Fagin about the failed robbery. He explained that they'd left Oliver, wounded and in a ditch.

On hearing this, Fagin rushed into the street and made straight for a public house. He asked if a man by the name of Monks was there.

But Fagin was in a hurry, and couldn't wait. Instead, he went to Sikes' house, and found Nancy lying with her head on the table. He made a noise, and she sat up.

Nancy couldn't bear to listen as Fagin said how much Oliver could earn for him by stealing. She shouted at Fagin.

As there was no sign of Sikes, Fagin left an emotional Nancy and returned home. He was just about to turn the key in the lock, when a dark figure whispered his name.

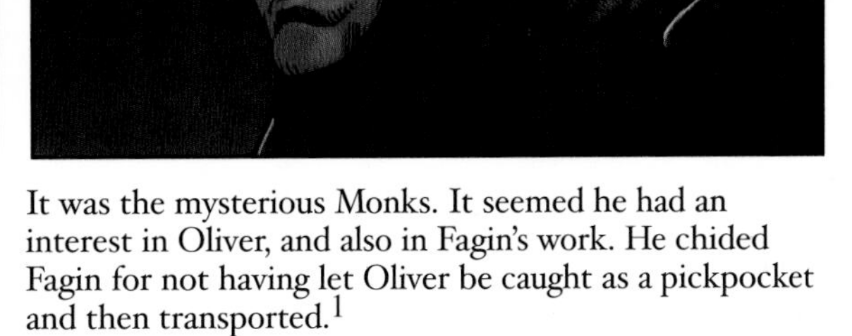

It was the mysterious Monks. It seemed he had an interest in Oliver, and also in Fagin's work. He chided Fagin for not having let Oliver be caught as a pickpocket and then transported.[1]

1. Transported: Criminals were sometimes sent to British colonies as punishment. See p.45 for more information.

A Change of Luck

All night, Oliver lay in the ditch, unable to move. The next day he stumbled toward a house, and made a noise at its door. It was the house he'd tried to burgle.

Oliver's knocks were heard, and no sooner had a servant carried him inside than he was recognized as one of the robbers!

The owner of the house, Mrs. Maylie, lived there with her niece, Rose. Mrs. Maylie said that Oliver was to be put to bed, and then she, Rose and Dr. Losberne sat at his bedside, waiting for him to wake.

It was the next morning before Oliver came to his senses. The occupants of the house listened as he told his story.

Rose was concerned for Oliver. She took pity on him, sure that he was not a bad child at all.

The police had been sent for, and when they saw the window used by the robbers, they came to a conclusion.

But Dr. Losberne convinced them that Oliver was not the same boy. He made up a story, saying that Oliver had simply had an accident.

1. Boyish trespass: Had an accident while playing.

Oliver was cared for by his new friends, and after many weeks he was well enough to leave his bed.

He had nothing but gratitude for Mrs. Maylie, Rose, and the kind-hearted Dr. Losberne. Oliver offered to serve them in any way he could, in order to repay their kindness to him.

But Oliver was also troubled by thoughts of Mr. Brownlow, whom he had left on an errand, and not returned to.

When Oliver was fully recovered from his injury, Dr. Losberne took him back to London, where it was hoped he would meet Mr. Brownlow. As their carriage drove along the city streets, Oliver turned pale as they passed Fagin's house, before carrying on in search of Mr. Brownlow's residence.

Oliver directed them to a white house. It was Mr. Brownlow's house, but a notice said it was empty.

They asked about Mr. Brownlow at the house next door, and learned he had gone to the West Indies. Oliver was filled with sadness at this news.

Oliver returned to Mrs. Maylie and Rose. After a few weeks he went with them to spend summer in a cottage in the countryside. He went on walks, and listened as Rose read from a book or played the piano. He had lessons and studied the Bible. Oliver had never been happier in all his life.

Faces at the window

After one particularly long walk, Rose was taken suddenly ill. As she lay in bed, her face as white as marble, Mrs. Maylie feared she might die.

Mrs. Maylie wrote a letter to Dr. Losberne, asking him to come at once. She told Oliver to take it to the post office in the nearby town.

The stranger was none other than Monks, the man who had shown so much interest in Oliver, but poor Oliver had no way to know this.

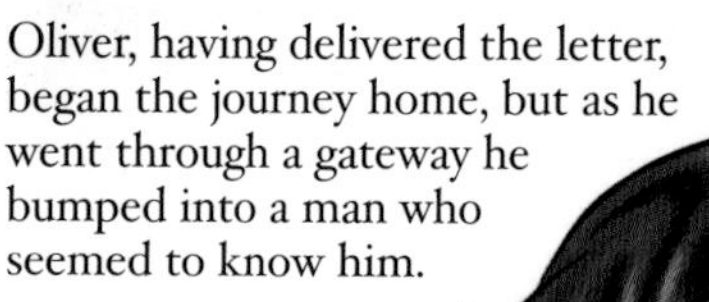

Oliver, having delivered the letter, began the journey home, but as he went through a gateway he bumped into a man who seemed to know him.

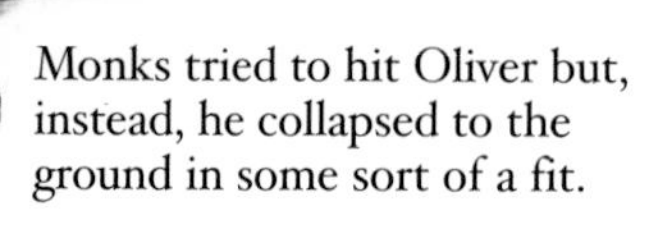

Monks tried to hit Oliver but, instead, he collapsed to the ground in some sort of a fit.

On receiving the news of Rose's illness, Dr. Losberne went to her. At first he feared that she was so gravely ill she would not recover. But slowly, Rose did recover from her fever.

While Rose recovered, Oliver applied himself to his studies. Each day he sat by a window reading his books. The room was on the ground floor at the back of the house, and one evening he fell fast asleep.

As he slept, he had a nightmare. He dreamt that Fagin and another man whose face was hidden were pointing at him and whispering. He awoke with a jump . . .

. . . and there, staring at him through the window, was indeed Fagin, and a man Oliver recognized as the stranger he'd bumped into in town: Monks!

Oliver cried out, and Mrs. Maylie's servant rushed into the room. The boy was in a most agitated state, pointing to the meadows behind the house and claiming he'd seen Fagin, his old tormentor, and another man.[1]

The servant set off in pursuit, but his search was in vain, as Fagin and Monks were nowhere to be seen. Back at the house, Oliver insisted that he hadn't been dreaming.

1. Agitated: Upset

A Secret is Overheard

One evening Mr. Bumble went to a pub. He met a stranger who was soon revealed as Monks, and who wanted information about Oliver's birth.

Mr. Bumble told Monks that the midwife died last winter, but his wife heard Sally's last words and could help. The next night Mrs. Corney (now Mrs. Bumble) met with Monks.

Monks handed over twenty-five pounds in gold coins for the secret the old midwife had told Mrs. Corney before she died.

As she gathered up the coins, she told how Oliver's mother had entrusted a gold locket to Sally. It would lead to the boy's true family who would care for him.

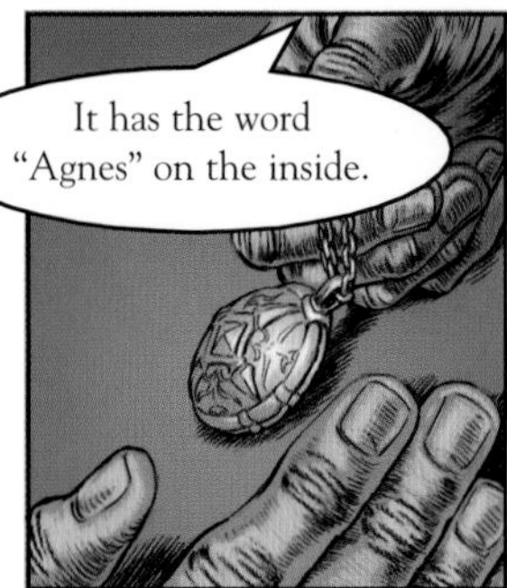

Mrs. Corney had the locket and, as she gave it to Monks, she explained what its contents were.

Monks examined the locket, its two locks of hair, a gold wedding ring, and a woman's name. He lifted a trapdoor, and threw them into the river below.

Monks went straight to Fagin, to tell him what he had learned about Oliver. The two thieves went to a quiet room, closed the door, and spoke in private.

Unknown to them, Nancy eavesdropped on their conversation, and heard their every word.[1]

After Monks had left, Fagin handed Nancy a bag of money owed to Sikes from the robberies they had done together. Nancy took it to Sikes.

1. Eavesdropped: Secretly listened to someone's conversation.

Sikes was ill, but he still scared Nancy. He sensed she was keeping something from him, and demanded to know what. As he fell into a deep sleep, Nancy crept out into the night.

Nancy went to the hotel where Rose Maylie was staying. She explained who she was and how she knew Oliver.

She told what she had heard at Fagin's—that Monks was Oliver's brother! As long as Oliver never knew this, Monks would inherit their family's fortune.

A while later, Oliver, who was with Rose in London, said he had spotted Mr. Brownlow entering a house.

Rose took Oliver to the house. He stayed in their carriage, while Rose explained to Mr. Brownlow how he had been the victim of misfortune.

Mr. Brownlow rushed from the room. He went to the carriage, and was reunited with Oliver. He brought Oliver into the house. Overjoyed, Oliver hugged Mrs. Bedwin, the housekeeper.

That evening, Mr. Brownlow called on Mrs. Maylie, who by now knew of Oliver's situation. They agreed to seek out Monks, so that Oliver could have what was rightly his—a share of his father's money.

MURDER!

At the beginning of this tale, we met two youths by the names of Noah Claypole and Charlotte, from Oliver's time as an undertaker's apprentice. This pair had now fled to London after robbing Mr. Sowerberry.

Looking for somewhere to stay, they chanced on a public house—the very place where Fagin lurked when he wanted fresh young recruits for his criminal gang.[1]

Fagin told the young couple they would be safe with him, and so Noah and Charlotte joined Fagin's gang.

It wasn't long before Fagin gave Noah a job to do. The Artful Dodger, who was Fagin's best hand, had been arrested for trying to pick a pocket, and was due in court.[2] Fagin sent Noah along to hear what punishment the judge had in store for him.

Noah hurried back to Fagin, and told him the Dodger's fate. Since Fagin's new recruit had served him so well, he was quick to find another job for him.

His task was to spy on Nancy, follow her wherever she went, see who she met, and eavesdrop on what she said. Everything that Noah discovered was to be reported back to Fagin.

1. Lurked: Waiting to do something secretive, often illegal.
2. Best hand: Best thief.

Late one night, Noah followed Nancy to London Bridge, where she met Mr. Brownlow and Rose.

Noah listened to Nancy's every word. She pleaded with them to spare Fagin and his gang, and then described Monks so they would recognize him.

Noah ran straight to Fagin to tell him what he had heard. Shortly after this, Sikes arrived with a bag of stolen goods, which he asked Fagin to sell for him.

But Fagin now had other things to think about. He made Noah repeat his story to Sikes, telling him exactly what he had seen and heard at London Bridge. Sikes was furious, as he realized Nancy had betrayed him.

Sikes returned to his house, locked the door after him and dragged a table in front of it. Then, waking Nancy from her sleep, he told her what he knew. The poor girl pleaded with Sikes to spare her, but his rage could not be stopped.

1. Extort the secret: To make Monks tell them the truth.

THE FATE OF SIKES

The brutal murder was done, and Sikes and his dog fled from London. He soon heard men talking about it, and knew he was a wanted man.

Sikes wandered for days. He tried to kill his dog, but it ran off. Sikes crept back to London, and went into hiding.

While Sikes was hiding like a rat, the police caught up with Fagin and Noah. Both were arrested and sent for trial before a jury.

An "arrest" of a different kind took place when Mr. Brownlow found Monks and took him back to his house for questioning.

The truth was soon out. Monks' real name was Edward Leeford, and Mr. Brownlow had been a good friend of his father's. In fact, Oliver and Monks were half-brothers because they had the same father but different mothers.

After the end of his loveless marriage to Monk's mother, their father fell in love with Agnes Fleming and planned to marry her. A rich relative died in Italy and Mr. Leeford went to claim his inheritance, but fell ill while away.

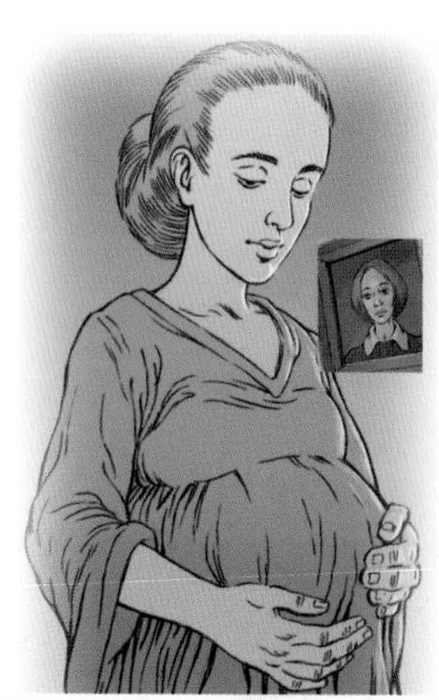

Oliver's father asked Mr. Brownlow to look after a portrait he'd painted of Agnes. He died before he could take it back.

When Monks' mother discovered her husband had left most of his money to Oliver, she burned his will, and so hid Oliver's true identity.

Meanwhile, in a squalid part of London, Sikes' hideaway was discovered. Soon a crowd had gathered to seek justice for Nancy's murder.

Sikes climbed onto the roof, taking a rope with him. He planned to lower himself to safety, but lost his balance and slipped over the edge.

The rope he had tied around the chimney caught around his neck, and tightened as he fell, forming a noose that broke his neck and jerked his body to a stop.

As Sikes' body swung on the rope, his dog, which had returned to its master, jumped from the roof to reach him, but howling, fell to the pavement and died.

OLIVER FINDS HIS FAMILY

Two days after the death of Sikes, Oliver travelled to the town of his birth in the company of Mrs. Maylie, Rose, and Mrs. Bedwin.

As the carriage neared the town, Oliver recognized familiar places, and pointed them out to Rose.

The carriage entered the town, and drove past the workhouse where Oliver was born and had spent his first years. They stopped at a hotel and after dinner, Mr. Brownlow arrived, bringing a man with him.

Oliver almost shrieked with surprise when he saw the man—the same man he had seen with Fagin staring at him through the window. Mr. Brownlow told Oliver the man was his brother.

Monks told Oliver that after their father had died, he and his mother had found the will, and a letter to Agnes. The letter was a confession that he could not marry Agnes because unknown to her, he was already married.

At this, Monks fell silent, so Mr. Brownlow continued the story. Leeford had left a small sum to Monks and his mother, but the majority of his wealth was split between Agnes and her child.

If the child was a boy, it would only inherit the money if it led a good life. If it fell into bad ways, then the money would go to the elder brother—Monks.

Oliver was stunned to hear how his own brother had paid Fagin to turn him into a criminal. In this way, Monks would get their father's money.

But the events of Oliver's past were not over yet, as Mr. Bumble and Mrs. Corney, his wife, were ushered into the room. Pointing to Monks, Mr. Brownlow asked them about their meeting in the pub.

Reluctantly, they confessed to their part in hiding Oliver's true identity. The story of how Mrs. Corney kept the locket belonging to Oliver's mother, and how she sold it to Monks, was told.

Mr. Brownlow went on. As Agnes was not married to Oliver's father, she fled her family in shame. Then, Mr. Brownlow said that Rose was Agnes' younger sister who Mrs. Maylie had taken pity on after her father died, and that she was therefore Oliver's aunt!

A New Beginning

At Fagin's trial a silence fell over the court as the jury returned its verdict: guilty. The judge, black cap on his head, sentenced him to death.

Alone in his dark cell in Newgate Prison, Fagin had time to think of all the wrongs he had ever done.[1] Suddenly frightenend, he banged on the door and walls, calling out for a candle.

A prison guard thrust a candle into a candlestick, and threw a mattress onto the cold stone floor.

On the day of his execution, Fagin was visited by Mr. Brownlow and Oliver. Mr. Brownlow demanded certain papers given to him by Monks.

Fagin asked Oliver to come closer to him. Oliver offered to say a prayer with Fagin, but the old thief still had cunning left in him.

Fagin pleaded with Oliver to help save him, but his fate was already sealed. The guards dragged Fagin, who struggled wildly, to the prison yard where he was to be hanged. His pitiful cries were left ringing in their ears.

1. Newgate Prison: Large prison in London where criminals were held before being executed.

Mr. Brownlow and Oliver left Newgate Prison. The papers Fagin had told them about would prove beyond any doubt who Oliver was. They passed Noah, who'd been released without charge. He had found a new career as an informer.[1]

As for Monks, he never did go back to calling himself by his real name, Edward Leeford. It was as Monks that he sailed to America where, falling once more into bad ways, he ended his days in a prison cell.

For Oliver, the orphaned boy from the workhouse who was taken in by thieves, there was a happy ending. His identity and his inheritance returned to him, he was adopted by Mr. Brownlow, who loved him as his own son.

Mr. Brownlow and Oliver moved away from London, and settled in the same country village where Mrs. Maylie and Rose lived. There was a small church in the village where Oliver and Rose would sometimes go, hand in hand.

Inside the church was a marble headstone to the memory of the mother Oliver never knew. The company of Rose and Mr. Brownlow was as close to perfect happiness as Oliver ever thought possible.

The End

1. Informer: A person who gives information about criminals to the police.

CHARLES DICKENS (1812-1870)

Charles John Huffam Dickens was born on February 7th, 1812, the eldest son of John and Elizabeth Dickens. Charles had only intermittent schooling, and in 1824, when he was 12, his father fell into debt. His father was sent to a debtor's prison and his mother and four younger brothers and sisters joined him, since there was nowhere else for them to live. As for Charles, because he was old enough to work, he was sent to earn money to provide for his family. He worked 12 hours a day gluing labels onto bottles of shoe polish. He lived in lodgings and walked four miles to work each day. He was only there for three months, but it made a lasting impression on him. It was a troubled time in the young boy's life.

EMPLOYMENT

When he was 15, Charles began work as an office boy at a firm of solicitors, and a year later he became a newspaper reporter. He enjoyed writing, and in 1833, when he was 21, he sent a short story to a magazine, which they printed. It marked the start of his career as an author. The magazine asked Charles to write more stories, which he did. Instead of writing under his own name, he used the pen name "Boz." His stories were popular with the magazine's readers, and in 1836 they were made into his first book, called *Sketches by Boz*.

Charles Dickens photographed in 1858 by Herbert Watkins Mary Evans Picture Library

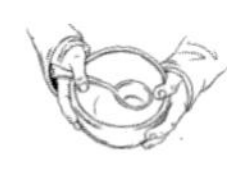

WHY "BOZ"?

"Boz" came from the name given to Charles' younger brother Augustus, who was originally nicknamed "Moses." The Dickens' children first turned this into "Boses" and then to "Boz." Charles must have liked the name enough to use it as his own pen name.

FAME

In February 1837, a new story by Charles began to appear each month in a magazine called *Bentley's Miscellany*, and the full title of his new story was *Oliver Twist*, or, *The Parish Boy's Progress*. Even though the story was by the mysterious "Boz," Charles was so famous after the success of *The Pickwick Papers* that everyone knew it was by him.

LATER LIFE

Charles devoted the rest of his life to writing. He toured Britain and America, giving readings from his books. He could be both funny and serious, and was able to draw attention to society's wrongs. He created larger-than-life characters that people either loved, like Mr. Micawber in *David Copperfield*, or loathed, like Fagin in *Oliver Twist*.

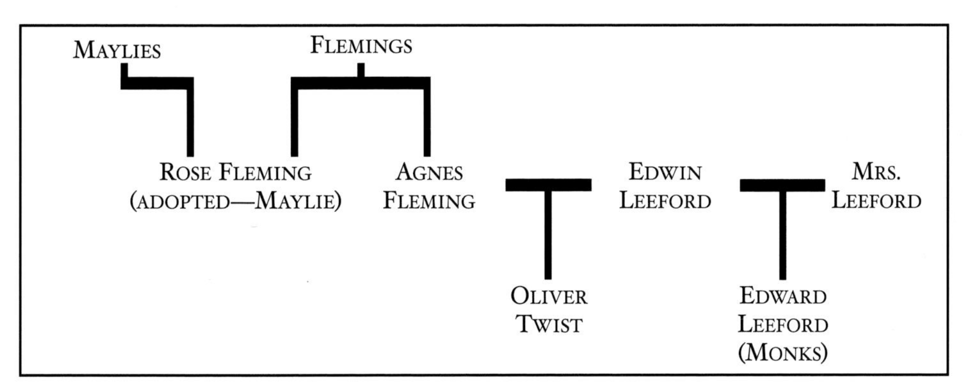

Illustration showing Oliver Twist's family tree.

OTHER BOOKS WRITTEN BY CHARLES DICKENS

1836—*Sketches by Boz*
1837—*The Pickwick Papers*
1838—*Oliver Twist*
1839—*Nicholas Nickleby*
1841—*The Old Curiosity Shop*
1841—*Barnaby Rudge*
1843—*A Christmas Carol*
1844—*Martin Chuzzlewit*
1845—*The Cricket on the Hearth*
1848—*Dombey and Son*
1850—*David Copperfield*
1853—*Bleak House*
1854—*Hard Times*
1857—*Little Dorrit*
1859—*A Tale of Two Cities*
1861—*Great Expectations*
1865—*Our Mutual Friend*
1870—*The Mystery of Edwin Drood* (unfinished at time of death).

Timeline of World Events

During the Lifetime of Charles Dickens

1812
February 7th—Born at 1 Mile End Terrace, Landport, Portsmouth, England, to John and Elizabeth Dickens.
Bankrupt banker assassinates British Prime Minister, Spencer Perceval, in the lobby of the British House of Commons.
War of 1812 begins between England and America.
Napoleon's troops enter Moscow but the retreating Russian troops burn the city.

1813
Westminster Bridge lit by gas fires for the first time.

1814
Charles' father (a naval pay clerk) is transferred to London.

1815
Battle of Waterloo.

1817
Father transferred to Chatham—family lives in Kent.

1820
George III dies. Succeeded by George IV.

1821
Charles starts school; becomes avid reader.

1824
Father is imprisoned in Marshalsea debtor's prison. The rest of his family also lived at Marshalsea during this time. Charles, aged 12, begins working at Warren's boot-blacking factory.

1827
Begins working as law clerk but doesn't enjoy it and pursues journalism instead.

1829
Metropolitan Police force founded. Succeeded the Bow Street Runners.

1830
William IV succeeds George IV on British throne.

1831–1833
Devastating cholera epidemic hits London killing as many as 7,000 people.

1834
Fire destroys Parliament.
Working as reporter for *Morning Chronicle.*
The Poor Law Amendment Act is passed—relief only available to poor people within a workhouse and these were deliberately made very uninviting to discourage people from entering. Men and women were separated and parents lost all right to see their children; all lived separately inside.

1836
Marries Catherine Hogarth.
First publication, *Sketches by Boz*, is published.
Invited by Richard Bentley to be first editor of his new magazine, *Bentley's Miscellany.*

1837
First novel, *The Pickwick Papers*, is published.
Victoria succeeds William IV on British throne.

1837–1839
Oliver Twist published in installments.

1839
Dickens argues with Richard Bentley and resigns as editor of *Bentley's Miscellany.*

1840
Rebuilding of Parliament completed.

1841
Dickens declines invitation to stand for Parliament.

1842
Mines Act bans the employment of women and children under 10 in the mines.

1845
Potato famine in Ireland.

1847
British Factory Act passed, restricting women and those between ages 13 and 18 to working no more than 10 hours per day.

1848
First Public Health Act sets up a Central Board to deal with public sewage, water supply and refuse.
First Gold Rush in California.

1850
Public Libraries Act creates free lending libraries.

1851
Dickens' father dies.
The Great Exhibition at Crystal Palace, Hyde Park, in London to celebrate both the success of the British Empire and advances in technology.

1854–1856
Crimean War between Russia and an allied Britain and France.

1854
Juvenile Offenders Act passed in Britain.
A second cholera epidemic hits Britain; Dr. John Snow begins work to prove that the disease is spread through dirty drinking water.

1858
Dickens is separated from his wife.

1861–1865
American Civil War.

1865
Train crash in Staplehurst, Kent, England—Dickens is in the only first class carriage not to be derailed. He helps the injured and dying, and then retrieves the unfinished manuscript of *Our Mutual Friend* from wreckage.

1868
British policy of transporting criminals to Australia and the colonies is abolished.

1869
Debtor's prisons abolished in Britain.

1870
June 9th—Dickens dies after a stroke.
June 14th—Buried in Poets Corner in Westminster Abbey.

Dickens Receiving His Characters, *from a painting by W.H. Beard, 1874*

London and the Poor

At the Time of Oliver Twist

Dickens wrote *Oliver Twist* in the 1830s, and set much of the action in London and the surrounding countryside. It was originally published as a serial, coming out in 27 monthly installments in the magazine *Bentley's Miscellany*, and then later as a three-volume book.

A West View of Newgate *by George Shepherd (1784–1862)*

London Divided

The middle-class readers of the magazine—and the book—were initially shocked, because Dickens was writing about a London they would hardly have known. He described the world of the poor, who were badly treated by society. He included pickpockets, thieves, and murderers, and took readers on a trip through London's dirty alleys and slums. These were exactly the people and places that readers of the story would probably have avoided at all costs—yet Dickens wanted them to experience the "other side" of London. In the 1830s, London's population was steadily increasing as people moved there in search of work. By the early 1840s two million people lived there. It was a city of opposites, separated by unbelievable poverty.

Rich and Poor

The wealthy lived in large, clean homes and had servants, but the poor were forced to live in over-crowded slums with several families sharing a house. The destitute poor—those who were so poor all they owned were the rags they stood up in—were sent to the workhouse. Employers had no problem finding workers to fill positions, so they began to reduce their workers' weekly wages—safe in the knowledge there was always someone willing to work for the little money they offered. It was not until the 1840s that a law was passed that children must attend school, and so children from poor families were often forced to work. Life was so hard that in 1840, the average life expectancy for a worker in Manchester was just 17 years.

Dickens understood the plight of the poor, and this is clear from his descriptions of the workhouse where Oliver Twist was born and raised. The government believed that workhouses were a solution to the problem of extreme poverty by providing food, shelter, and work for the poor in society. In truth, the workhouse system simply kept the poor off the streets, deprived them of their dignity, and split families apart. Workhouses had separate quarters for men, women, and children. They were little more than prisons for people too poor, too old, or too weak to care for themselves.

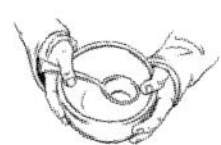

A Law the Poor Hated

Dickens wrote *Oliver Twist* at a time when conditions for the poor were changing. In 1834, the government passed the Poor Law Amendment Act. The Act said the poor would only receive relief (food and shelter) if they agreed to accept the strict rules of a workhouse which, after 1834, came under the control of a board of officials. A board was usually made up of magistrates and ministers of the Church of England. Conditions inside a workhouse were deliberately harsh. The idea was to persuade people not to be poor in the first place. The law met with great opposition, and was loathed by the poor.

The workhouse system described by Dickens in *Oliver Twist* is based entirely on the 1834 Act. He introduced readers to the strict rules of the workhouse, the punishments, the harsh conditions, and the people in charge. Dickens wrote about things he thought people should know about and wanted to make people aware of inequalities in society.

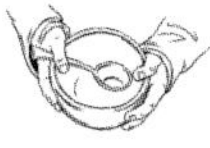

Crime and Punishment

During the 17th and 18th centuries, "transportation" was seen as a means of punishing common crimes such as theft that would otherwise have carried a death sentence. Many convicts were sent to the British colonies in America until the Revolutionary War and a newly-independent America stopped the practice. Therefore, after 1787, transported convicts were sent to New South Wales in Australia. The journey meant many months at sea, locked in small and overcrowded cages; many died during the voyage. Even if they survived the journey, served their sentence, and were granted a pardon, many people never saw their homes or families again.

Oliver Through the Ages

From Serial to the Silver Screen

Dickens used slang which he researched thoroughly to ensure it was an accurate portrayal of how figures from the criminal underworld would have talked. He often used characters' speech as it was spoken, rather than using the standard spelling—this is called a *colloquialism*.

Serial Novels

Oliver Twist was originally published in monthly installments in *Bentley's Miscellany* from January 1837 until April 1839. One possible reason why many of his novels are so long is that the longer the serial continued, the more he got paid. Serialization meant that the serials were cheap to buy and so were read by a large number of people, with cliff-hangers keeping people buying. Each installment of *Oliver Twist* was approximately 9,000 words long, and Dickens wrote around two of these each month.

A Social Conscience

The novel cleverly shows the gap between the rich and the poor. Oliver was born into poverty; it was very unlikely that he would ever escape from this, and he was lucky to be found by the wealthy Mr. Brownlow.

The "Stop, thief!" scene from Roman Polanski's Oliver Twist, *2005 TopFoto.co.uk*

The reader is shown the heartless and uncaring attitudes of the workhouse officials, and Dickens also shows the cruelty of selling children to brutal employers such as the Sowerberrys.

Controversy

Critics debated the issue of "appropriateness" for the respectable people. "There is a sort of Radicalish tone about *Oliver Twist* that I don't altogether like," wrote one critic. Novelist William Thackeray, a rival of Dickens, asserted that men of genius "had no business to make these characters interesting or agreeable, to be feeding their readers' morbid fancies, or indulging their own, with such monstrous food."

Royal Fans

It was hugely popular and led to many discussions—even the new queen, Victoria, had read it, although she said she disapproved of it for younger readers. The prime minister, Lord Melbourne, said: "all about workhouses and coffin makers and pickpockets . . . I don't like that low and debasing view of mankind." Even those who couldn't afford to buy the novel in its entirety could read it in installments.

A Publishing Revolution

The success of *Oliver Twist* had a huge impact on Victorian publishing. *Nicholas Nickleby*, Dickens' next serialized novel, was first published before *Oliver Twist* had even finished, and sold an incredible 50,000 copies on its first day of publication. After this, all of Dickens' later novels and many of his contemporaries—including William Thackeray, George Eliot, Joseph Conrad, and Thomas Hardy—were serialized.

What the Critics Said

From *The Edinburgh Review, or Critical Journal*: For October 1838–January 1839

"We think him a very original writer—well entitled to his popularity" " . . . we know no writer who seems likely to attain higher success in that rich and useful department of fiction which is founded on faithful representations of human character."

Film and Stage

1948—A film version directed by David Lean and starring Alec Guinness as Fagin is released and becomes a critical success.
1960—*Oliver!* A musical version written by Lionel Bart opens in London.
1968—*Oliver!* the musical is turned into a film—it wins six Oscars in 1969, including Best Picture and Best Director.
2005—Oscar-winning director, Roman Polanski's *Oliver Twist* is released starring Ben Kingsley as Fagin.
The musical version may be the best known, but is a much more light-hearted adaptation than Dickens would have intended.

INDEX

IF YOU LIKED THIS BOOK, YOU MIGHT ALSO WANT TO TRY THESE TITLES IN THE BARRON'S *GRAPHIC CLASSICS* SERIES:

Treasure Island
Moby Dick
The Hunchback of Notre Dame
Kidnapped
Journey to the Center of the Earth

FOR MORE INFORMATION ON CHARLES DICKENS:

The Dickens Museum
www.dickensmuseum.com

The Victoria and Albert Museum
www.vam.ac.uk